ready, steady, read!

Hedgehogs Don't Eat Hamburgers

Vivian French
Illustrated by Chris Fisher

Puffin Books

PUFFIN BOOKS

Published by the Penguin Group
Penguin Books Ltd, 27 Wrights Lane, London W8 5TZ, England
Penguin Books USA Inc., 375 Hudson Street, New York, New York 10014, USA
Penguin Books Australia Ltd, Ringwood, Victoria, Australia
Penguin Books Canada Ltd, 10 Alcorn Avenue, Toronto, Ontario, Canada M4V 3B2
Penguin Books (NZ) Ltd, 182–190 Wairau Road, Auckland 10, New Zealand

Penguin Books Ltd, Registered Offices: Harmondsworth, Middlesex, England

Published in Puffin Books 1993
10 9 8 7 6 5 4

Filmset in Monotype Bembo Schoolbook

Reproduction by Anglia Graphics Ltd, Bedford

Made and printed in Great Britain by William Clowes Ltd, Beccles and London

Contents

HEDGEHOGS DON'T EAT HAMBURGERS

Hector saw a picture on a paper bag.

"What's that?" he asked.

"That's a hamburger," said his dad.

"Can I have one for my tea?"
asked Hector.

"No," said his dad. "Hedgehogs
don't eat hamburgers."

"I do," said Hector. "And I'm
going to go and find one for my
tea."

Hector set off to find a hamburger.

"Here I go, here I go, here I
go," he sang as he walked along.

Hattie popped out to see who
was going by.

"Hello," said Hector. "I'm
going to find my tea."

"Would you like some fine fat
snails?" Hattie asked.

"No thank you," said Hector.
"I'm going to find a hamburger."

"Hedgehogs don't eat
hamburgers," said Hattie.

"I do," said Hector.

"Oh," said Hattie. "Maybe I'll
come too."

So she did.

Hector and Hattie set off to find a hamburger.

"Here we go, here we go, here we go," they sang as they walked along.

Harry popped out to see who was going by.

"Hello," said Hector. "We're going to find my tea."

"Would you like some slow slimy slugs?" Harry asked. "I've got plenty."

"No thank you," said Hector.
"I'm going to find a hamburger."

"Hedgehogs don't eat
hamburgers," said Harry.

"I do," said Hector.

"Oh," said Harry. "Maybe I'll
come too."

So he did.

Hector and Hattie and Harry set off to find a hamburger.

"Here we go, here we go, here we go," they sang as they walked along.

Hester popped out to see who was going by.

"Hello," said Hector. "We're going to find my tea."

"Would you like some big black beetles?" Hester asked. "I've got lots."

"No thank you," said Hector.

"I'm going to find a hamburger."

"Hedgehogs don't eat hamburgers," said Hester.

"I do," said Hector.

"Oh," said Hester. "Maybe I'll come too."

So she did.

Hector and Hattie and Harry and Hester set off to find a hamburger.

"Here we go, here we go, here we go," they sang as they walked along.

Fox popped out to see who was going by.

"Hello," said Hector. "We're going to find my tea."

"Tea, eh?" said Fox. "What a good idea." He looked at the fat little hedgehogs, and he licked his lips.

"I'm going to find a hamburger," said Hector.

"WHAT a good idea," said Fox. "Shall I show you the way?"

"YES PLEASE," said Hector.

Hector and Hattie and Harry and
Hester set off after Fox.

"Here we go, here we go, here
we go," they sang as they walked
along.

"SSSHHH!" said Fox.

"Oh," said Hector and Hattie
and Harry and Hester.

They walked up the hill and
down the hill.

"Are we nearly there?" asked
Hector.

"Nearly," said Fox. He sniffed
the air. "Yes, we're nearly there."

Hector sniffed the air too.
"What is it?" he asked.

"That's the smell of the town,"
said Fox. "That's where the
hamburgers are."

"Oh," said Hector. He sniffed the air again. He could smell cars, and smoke, and shops, and houses. He could smell danger. "Maybe I don't want a hamburger today. Maybe I'll have big black beetles, or slow slimy slugs, or fine fat snails. Maybe hedgehogs don't eat hamburgers after all."

Hector turned round, and Hattie and Harry and Hester all turned round too.

"Here we go, here we go, here we go!" they sang.

"JUST A MINUTE," said Fox,
and he opened his mouth wide.
His teeth were sharp and white.
"What about MY tea?"

"YOU can have a hamburger,"
said Hector.

"But I don't WANT a hamburger," said Fox. "I want little fat HEDGEHOGS!" And he jumped at Hector and Hattie and Harry and Hester.

"HERE WE GO, HERE WE GO, HERE WE GO," sang all four little hedgehogs, and they rolled themselves up tightly into four prickly balls.

"OWWWW!" said Fox as he hurt his nose. "OW! OW! OW!" He turned round and ran up the hill and down the hill. He didn't stop running until he got home to his mummy.

Hector and Hattie and Harry and
Hester looked at each other.

"Let's go home," said Hector.

So they all set off to go home.

"Home we go, home we go,
home we go," they sang as they
walked up the hill and down the
hill. And they got home just in
time to have fine fat snails,
slow slimy slugs and
big black beetles for
their tea.

THE HEDGEHOGS' SONG

The sun was going down in the
sky, and the birds were singing
their last songs. Hector was
singing too.

"SSSH!" said his dad.

"What are you doing?" asked
Hector.

"Listening," said his dad.

"Oh," said Hector. "What for?"

"I'm listening for things that
wriggle," said his dad.

"Things that wriggle are
sometimes big and sometimes little.
Sometimes they are dangerous, but
sometimes they are good to eat.
Wriggly white grubs are VERY
good to eat."

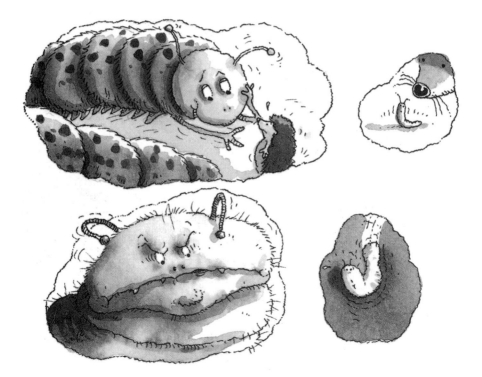

"Shall I sing you my song?" asked
Hector. "Then you can listen to
me instead. It's a song about Big
Bad Badger."

"Hush!" said his dad. "You must always be polite to Badger, or he might fancy YOU for his tea."

"Not me," said Hector. "I'm MUCH too clever."

Hector went to see Hattie. Hattie was sitting under a beech tree, where the dry leaves lay thickly on the ground.

"What are you doing?" he asked.

"Listening," said Hattie.

"Oh," said Hector. "What for?"

"I'm listening for things that rustle," said Hattie. "Things that rustle are sometimes big and sometimes little. Sometimes they are dangerous, but sometimes they are good to eat."

"Shall I sing you my song?" Hector said. "Then you can listen to me instead."

"All right," said Hattie.

Hector sang,

> "Big bad badger
> Looking for his tea.
> Pull his tail, make him wail
> One two three!"

"That's nice," said Hattie. "Let's go and sing it to Harry."

Hector and Hattie went to see Harry. Harry was sitting under a bramble bush, where the blackberries grew.

"What are you doing?" they asked.

"Listening," said Harry.

"Oh," said Hector. "What for?"

"I'm listening for things that creep," said Harry. "Things that creep are sometimes big and sometimes little. Sometimes they are dangerous, but sometimes they are good to eat."

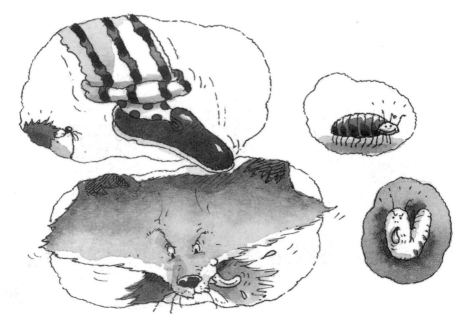

"Shall we sing you a song?" asked
Hector. "Then you can listen to us
instead."

"All right," said Harry.

So Hector and Hattie sang their
song.

"That's nice," said Harry, when
they had finished singing. "Let's
go and sing it to Hester."

Hector and Hattie and Harry
went to see Hester. Hester was
standing near an old stone wall.

"What are you doing?" they
asked.

"Listening," said Hester.

"Oh," said Hector. "What for?"

"I'm listening for things that slither," said Hester. "Things that slither are sometimes big and sometimes little. Sometimes they are dangerous, but sometimes they are good to eat."

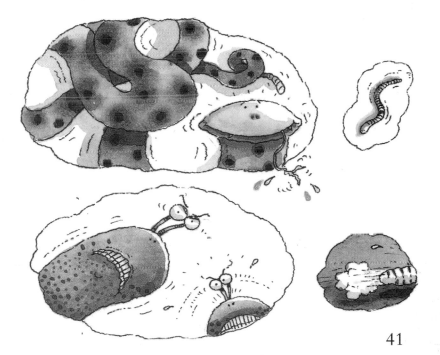

"Shall we sing you a song?" asked
Hector. "Then you can listen to us
instead."

"All right," said Hester.

So Hector and Hattie and
Harry sang their song.

"That's nice," said Hester. "Let's
go and sing it while we walk
through the woods."

Hector and Hattie and Harry and Hester sang as they walked through the woods.

"Big bad badger
Looking for his tea.
Pull his tail, make him wail
One two three!"

They walked under the beech
trees, where the dry leaves lay
thick on the ground. Big things
and little things rustled in the
leaves, but Hector and Hattie and
Harry and Hester didn't hear
them.

They walked under the bramble
bushes, where the blackberries
grew. Big things and little things
were creeping all around, but
Hector and Hattie and Harry and
Hester didn't hear them.

They walked along beside
the old stone wall.

Big things and little things
slithered up and down it, but
Hector and Hattie and Harry and
Hester didn't hear them.

"Let's sing our song to the
birds," said Hector.

They climbed right up to the top
of the wall and began to sing.

"Big bad badger," sang Hector
and Hattie and Harry and Hester.

Hester heard a noise, and
looked down. "Oh!" she said, and

stopped singing.

"Looking for his tea," sang
Hector and Hattie and Harry.

Hattie heard a noise, and
looked down. "Oh!" she said, and
stopped singing.

"Pull his tail, make him wail,"
sang Hector and Harry.

Harry heard a noise and looked
down. "Oh!" he said, and stopped
singing.
"ONE TWO THREE!" sang
Hector, at the top of his voice.

"WHAT a noisy little
hedgehog!" said a very loud voice
from the bottom of the wall.

"OH!" said Hector. "OH!...
Hello, Mr Badger."

Badger looked up at Hector and
Hattie and Harry and Hester.

"I'm very fond of a song," he
said. "Sing your song to me."

"If you say so, Mr Badger,"
said Hector.

"I do," said Badger. "And hurry
up about it."

Hector began to sing.

"Big brave badger
Looking for his tea.
Caught a snail, made it wail
One two three!"

"I see," said Badger. "And are
you sure that it wasn't a silly little
hedgehog that was caught?"

Hector shook his head. "Not this
time, Mr Badger," he said.
"And next time I'll be looking
out."

"Next time," said Badger, "you might not be on the top of a wall." And he turned and trotted away.

"Phew!" said Hector.

"I want to go home," said Hattie.

"Me too," said Harry.

"And me," said Hester.

"Shall we sing my song?" Hector
asked.

"NO!" said Hattie and Harry
and Hester.

They went home very quietly.
They climbed back down the wall
and they heard big and little
things slithering beside them.

They crept under the bramble
bushes and they heard big things
and little things creeping all
around them.

They tiptoed under the beech
trees and they heard big things
and little things rustling with them
through the dry leaves.

Hector's dad was waiting for him.
"You can sing your song to me
now," he said. "I've caught plenty
of wriggly white grubs for our
dinner."

"All right," said Hector.

He sang,

"Clever little hedgehogs
Looking all around.
Tiptoe here and tiptoe there
Never make a sound!"

Hector went indoors to eat
wriggly white grubs, and Hattie
and Harry and Hester tiptoed all
the way home.

ready, steady, read!